A Christmas
Far From Home

or

Charlie's Tragedy:
the Christmas Special

Published by Briny Bindings.

Printed POD by IngramSpark and affiliates, USA.

Author: Tallmadge Swartzfager
Art and Heart: Michaella Saccullo
Editor: Tallmadge Swartzfager (Caleb Toth also read it)
Layout, Design, Formatting: Tallmadge Swartzfager

ISBN: 979-8-8693-8390-7

A Lamplighter Underground Book

A Christmas Far From Home

or

Charlie's Tragedy: the Christmas Special

Written by:
Tallmadge Swartzfager

Illustrated and
Inspired by:
Michaella Saccullo

Pas-de-Calais,
Northern France

*   *   *

24th December, 1914

It had finally fallen quiet. The silence fell with the snowflakes. Someone tapped Jack on the shoulder.

"Head down, Jacko," said a voice, "I'll keep an eye on 'em."

Jack slid down from the parapet and his head sank into his arms. He shivered, and his exhausted body refused to sleep. The numbness of cold and war and fatigue all mingled together, but having been ignored for so long, he was now insensible to it — numb to the numbness.

"Mail, Jack," someone else laid a hand on his shoulder, "mail is here."

Feet crunched away through an icy trench. Jack stirred himself, stepped off the platform, and tramped his way up the line. The clouds in the sky high above were dark and dusky in the twilight, black streaked with purple by the setting sun. The veil had been pulled; the heavens could no longer bear to look upon the torn, mud-churned earth where God's children slaughtered each other with bullets and shells. The angels were weeping up there, beyond that veil, but the hearts of men were so cold and hard the tears froze before they could reach the ground. Already a thin layer of white had dusted everything — trench, field, coats, hats, guns, cannons.

No one made a sound as Jack walked past. A few whispered conversations went on furtively, but when the wind of Jack's passing whispered slightly lounder, these fell silent in deference. It was not Jack himself who had this effect. It was the sadness perhaps, or the lunacy, or the spirit of the gloaming: silence. Men lay curled in dugouts, huddled around fires, paced and stamped quietly, looked up at the sky, down at the ground, at the faces around them. Nobody said a word.

Jack's feet were cold. So cold. Colder than anything had ever been before. So cold the tears of the angels froze into snow and heaven pulled a veil before its eyes. Jack stopped and slumped against the frost-studded boards of the trench wall, and cried. Quiet tears which stung against his skin flowed haltingly, striving to remain warm — but still they froze somewhat to his face. It was the sadness, and the lunacy, and the silence; so he cried. A man can weep, and when a mother or a lover dies he shall, but Jack cried. Little boys will cry when they are frightened or hurt. He was frightened, and he was hurting; so he cried.

Someone stopped next to him. "Chin up, soldier," the officer said not unkindly, "when I was a boy, away from my family, I grew homesick when things were quiet. It made me crave the noise and rush. Don't — don't crave the cannons and the violence."

Jack nodded and wiped the tears away. When he looked up the officer was already gone, a tall, broad-shouldered presence pacing slowly down the trench, strong and encouraging. Jack stumbled on. Finally he came to an intersection, and heading left he moved away from the front and followed a zigzagging path until he came to a door on the left-hand side. Over it was carved in a board and stained with an attempt at home-made paint, *Rose Court, No. 1435a/b Dover Way*. Jack pushed the door open.

"Jack, Jack, you're back!"

Jack smiled weakly at his cousin Vibert, even while Charlie and Toby both leapt forward to shut the door and dust the snowflakes off of Jack's cap and shoulders.

"Hey all," he said.

"How's the front?" asked Tommy from his bunk where he lay with his blankets pulled up under his chin.

"All quiet," replied Jack while Charlie helped him out of his coat, "I heard the mail had come."

Rose Court was one of the happier, cleaner, and brighter holes in northern France. Jack, the eldest of the five residents, was the one who had assembled this group of fine young men. Vibert, his Aunt Madeline's younger son, was his closest cousin; while on the other side of his family, Toby was his first cousin by his Uncle Victor, and Charlie and Tommy were both second cousin's by Toby's mother Aunt Leah. So it was that the five of them, each with his own surname, had come to live in the same dugout on the left-hand side of a trench ten yards from the front.

Charlie hung Jack's coat on the pegs, next to Colonel Joseph's coat. Colonel Joseph's coat had one task in this world, and that was to hang on that peg. Once the inhabitants of No. 1435a/b Dover Way had been six, but now they were five. Colonel Joseph had been the only inmate at Rose Court not related even by marriage to any of the others. Now all his earthly relations and obligations had ceased, and his coat hung by the door as empty as his seat around the family table in back home in Rotherham.

"It did indeed," said Vibert, flapping a letter he held in his hands, "you got a little something yourself." He motioned to a package sitting on the meager table in the center of their living space.

"Poor Vibert," teased Tommy, "always jealous that Polly's love for him fits in an envelope while Daisy's love for Jack has to be squeezed into a parcel."

Vibert rolled his eyes and busied himself with his letter.

"Never make fun of a married man," warned Jack, cutting the string on his package. He pulled out a note and started reading, a smile cracking his face.

"What's that face for?" asked Vibert, peaking over the edge of his own letter. "Let me see what you got!"

"Get back, Vibert!" Jack mock-snapped at him, snatching up a little tin that sat nestled in the middle of the package, "this isn't yours to share!"

"Fudge!" gasped Tommy, ripping the covers back and leaping from his bunk.

"How do you know it's fudge?" demanded Vibert, even as he helped his distant relation corner Jack.

"Lucky guess," said Jack, one corner of his mouth tugging up, "but according to the date on this note," he added, looking down at it again, "it's already stale."

"Daisy makes the best stale fudge I ever tasted," insisted Tommy.

"Tommy, quit begging like a dog," said Toby, "you're a disgrace."

"No," corrected the youngest cousin, "I'm enjoying my youth, or what's left of it."

Jack shouldn't have, but he took out a piece of fudge and tossed it to Tommy. Tommy retreated gleefully to his bunk and nibbled away at it slowly.

"If you leave crumbs ..." began Toby.

"The rats have to eat too, Toby," smiled Charlie, "don't be uncharitable, cousin." Jack tossed each of them a piece too.

"You really shouldn't encourage him, Jack," said Vibert around the corner of his own piece of fudge, "it's very unhelpful to his development and rather beneath your character as a married man. You're setting up bad patterns for forming the habits and behaviors of sons."

Jack cocked an eyebrow. "Am I, as a *married man*?"

Vibert winked and grinned.

They all chewed their fudge in silence and read their respective letters. Charlie balanced his on one knee while tenderly treating his John Brown Belt with leather oil. Toby likewise was polishing every piece of brass on not only his own uniform but also everyone else's. Clothes make the man, and there was not a better groomed fire team in the entire British Army. "Look sharp, feel sharp; feel sharp, be sharp," as Major Sipe always said, to which Tommy would add under his breath, "Be sharp, shoot sharp."

A chill passed through Jack, and he asked Vibert to throw a little coal in the stove. Vibert did so.

"It never was worth making plans."

"What?"

"It never was worth making plans, was it?" repeated Vibert, "When everything I thought I would be doing, and everything I was doing, was arrested by … the war."

Shhh! said Toby, "don't mention the sadness."

"I wouldn't call it a sadness, Toby," Charlie said in a very reasonable sort of voice, "it's certainly not a holiday, but it's not a *tragedy*. Just think, we have a chance to serve both king and country here — and the Belgians are already outdoing us, breaking their own dikes and flooding the countryside to stop the Germans."

"Comedy ends in a wedding," quoted Vibert absentmindedly, "tragedy in death."

Charlie began to make matches in his head for his two unmarried cousins.

"It's too quiet," said Tommy, looking up as if he expected an artillery shell to suddenly come crashing down upon them.

"Vibert!" Jack leapt to his feet as if he'd sat on a tack and scattered his open tin of fudge across the rude dirt floor.

"Jack!" The boys could have wept for the loss.

"Vibert! O, boys! O, boys!"

"What is it Jack? Contain yourself, man! What's wrong?"

"Absolutely nothing is wrong!" Jack was dancing about while Tommy dove back and forth trying to salvage perfectly good stale fudge. "I'm going to be a father!"

"Daisy is … with child?!?"

"Uncle Toby!" exclaimed Charlie, clapping his cousin on the back. Toby beamed.

"This calls for a celebration!" said Tommy, sticking a piece of fudge in his mouth like a cigar and tossing a few more to his brethren.

Vibert's bounced off his chest as he fairly jumped on top of Jack. "Jack, oh Jack! Congratulations! We have to tell Emmie! And Polly! I'll have to write Polly immediately, a whole separate letter — no wait, I better send her a telegram —"

"Uncle Vibert, calm down, think!" laughed Jack as Charlie, Toby, and Tommy began a rousing chorus in celebration. "Even if the mail had been delivered on time," it never was, "they would have known before these letters reached us."

"Oh … well, I have to tell someone!" insisted Vibert, and then springing over to the door he threw it open and shouted, "Jack's going to be a father and I'm going to be an uncle!" before slamming it shut again.

Jack laughed, but there was a tear in his eye. Precious little in the way of the already scant good news they received here could have induced even Vibert to

break the sacred silence of the trenches, and while Jack rejoiced in that joy itself alone, not to mention the gladsome tidings of his wife's letter, remembering the silence brought back all the reality of the world around him, a world of mud, blood, shells, eternal thunder, sickness, murder, and sadness.

"What are you going to name him, Jack?" Vibert bounced on his toes.

"How do you know it's a he?"

"Just a guess."

"'Hope springs eternal,' doesn't it," Jack grinned again and winked at the others, "but Daisy will never consent to naming her child after my favorite cousin Vibert. But then, I won't have much say in what to name the child, will I?" Jack hardly wanted to fight the sadness. "Daisy will have to begin her motherhood alone."

"Not alone," said Vibert, calming himself and speaking very earnestly to his cousin, "she'll have her mother, and Polly, and Emmie, besides cousin Margery and May and Kate and Susan and everyone else."

"The war can't last forever," piped in Charlie, "it will end soon enough, come springtime I'm sure, and we'll all go home."

"You're right, boys," sighed Jack.

"I'm going to write to Polly to advocate for naming the child after his uncle," Vibert said, turning to collect paper and pen to the table.

"Polly put the kettle on?" quoted Tommy.

"Shut up, Tommy," Vibert turned around, half serious.

"I believe," Charlie smiled and sat up straight, "that is the first time in my life I've heard those words without their being directed at *me*!" Then his eyes widened and he shuddered.

"Isn't natural, is it?" asked Toby.

Each with his letters to read and to write, the boys settled in quietly to their work. Soon the only sounds to be heard were the scratch of pens and the ticking of pocket watches. Then a third sound entered the room, and Vibert and Jack both glanced up to see Tommy fast asleep. They grinned at each other; Jack returned to his reading and Vibert checked his watch.

Vibert sighed — that was the signal for the evening toilet to begin. Toby and Charlie joined him in jogging papers together and laying them aside, brushing teeth, putting coal in the little stove, putting boots and rifles in a row, saying their nightly prayers — Jack was oblivious, listening to Daisy's voice as longing eyes lingered over every letter of every word she had written him.

"Goodnight, Jack."

Jack looked up, half startled, half inquisitive. Vibert was standing there, looking down at him.

"Goodnight, Vibert."

"Sleep well, gentlemen," said Charlie from his bed, "pleasant dreams."

There was a pounding on the door, and before the boys were fully awake they had already pulled on boots, leapt out of bed, and thrown their John Browns over their shoulders. The door swung open and a head stuck itself in.

"Jacko, there's something going on. Come take a look. All of you be ready," it added before vanishing.

Without a word they all pulled on coats, tugged on caps, grabbed rifles, and bustled out the door. If there was danger, they would all face it together. And if all there was today was bitter cold as yesterday and more silence, this too they would bear together.

Utter silence still reigned over the trenches, yet there was a low bustle as men hastened quickly and quietly to ready positions. The grey of predawn revealed a muted version of an already depressingly monochromatic world. The five cousins came to a halt before a platform against the parapet. Here an officer stood with two soldiers; the soldiers stooped, as if worried to stand too tall even in the quiet and the stillness, while the officer arched his back a little to peer over the edge of the trench across no-man's-land, a disregarded periscope leaning next to him.

Jack didn't say a word. One of the soldiers beside the officer hopped down, and Jack climbed up where he had been, peering out of the trench with the officer.

"What do you make of it, corporal?"

Everyone listened closely.

"A Christmas tree, sir."

"Get out of the way," Vibert hopped up onto the shooting bench and elbowed past the cowering soldier before sticking his brow over the parapet. A moment later the others followed, Charlie, Tommy, Vibert, the officer, Jack, and Toby all in a row.

Just as Jack said, there was clearly a Christmas tree just before the German trench. It was not very large, not very ornate, but it was beautiful, lit with a few candles and bedecked with simple ornaments of paper and scrap tin, the chain of a pocket watch — and all along the edge of no-man's-land, that far, haunting, accursed edge of no-man's-land, there were candles, and lanterns

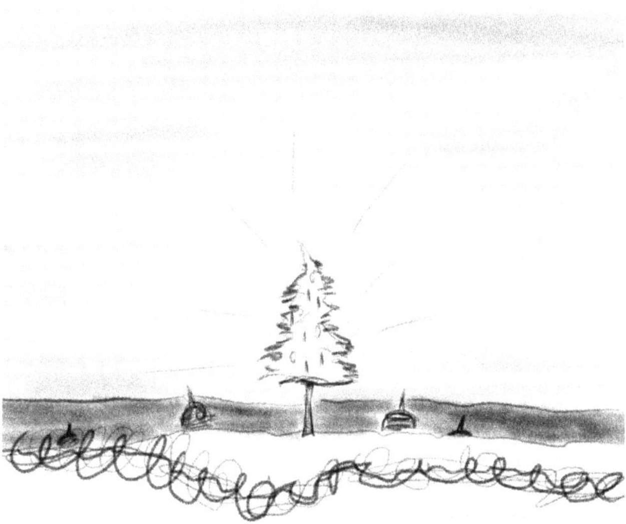

"A Christmas tree, sir."

wrapped in colored paper and foils, little decorations, a nutcracker, and another little tree far to the left, and another farther to the right.

"O! Happy Christmas!" Charlie wrapped his arms around Tommy, "I almost forgot!"

"Happy Christmas, Charlie — get off!" Tommy wriggled loose and straightened his ruffled uniform.

Then voices began to sing.

O Tannenbaum, O Tannenbaum,
Wie treu sind deine Blätter
O Tannenbaum, O Tannenbaum
Wie treu sind deine Blätter
Du grünst nicht nur zur Sommerzeit
Nein, auch im Winter, wenn es schneit
O Tannenbaum, O Tannenbaum
Wie treu sind deine Blätter

O Tannenbaum, O Tannenbaum
Du kannst mir sehr gefallen
O Tannenbaum, O Tannenbaum
Du kannst mir sehr gefallen
Wie oft hat nicht zur Winterzeit
Ein Zweig von dir mich hoch erfreut
O Tannenbaum, O Tannenbaum
Du kannst mir sehr gefallen
Du grünst nicht nur zur Sommerzeit
Nein, auch im Winter, wenn es schneit

O Tannenbaum, O Tannenbaum
Wie treu sind deine Blätter

O Tannenbaum, O Tannenbaum
Wie treu sind deine Blätter

All along the British line, men were peaking over the thin layer of dirt that separated life from death. Snow clung to the barbed wire, but the lights from the German line shone through it all with a friendly glow.

"Oh how lovely!" said Charlie, who had joined with the singing, "let's sing one back! We all know *Silent Night.*"

"Wait!" said the officer.

A solitary figure had risen from the German trench, arms raised and hands empty, illuminated by the little Christmas tree.

"We are all friends!" they heard him shout, "you no shoot we, we no shoot you."

"We are all friends!" came a chorus of accented calls from the trench behind him.

"Huns," spat the officer, but before he could say anything more Charlie vaulted out of the trench and began to sing.

Silent night, holy night,
All is calm, all is bright,
Round yon Virgin — Mother and Child;
Holy infant, so tender and mild,
Sleep in heavenly peace,
Sleep in heavenly peace.

Silent night, holy night,
Son of God, love's pure light,
Radiant beams from Thy holy face
With the dawn of redeeming grace;
Jesus Lord, at Thy birth,
Jesus Lord, at Thy birth!

Even as he sang, the German turned, spoke a few words down into his trench, and began to conduct with his arms.

> *Stille Nacht, heilige Nacht*
> *Alles schläft; einsam wacht*
> *Nur das traute hochheilige Paar.*
> *Holder Knabe im lockigen Haar,*
> *Schlaf in himmlischer Ruh!*
> *Schlaf in himmlischer Ruh!*

Vibert and Toby jumped up after Charlie and began singing, Tommy and Jack climbing after them, all five ignoring the protests, curses, and orders of the officer. When the song finished, Charlie began to pick his way gingerly through the wire, calling, "We are all friends!" In response dozens of Germans came over the top, empty hands waving, calling out, "We are all friends!" and "No shoot, no shoot!"

The German officer waded into the tangle of barbed-wire to meet Charlie, and there in the middle of no-man's-land they shook hands.

"Oh!" said Jack, remembering something, "the fudge, Tommy, go back and get the fudge!"

Tommy snapped a smart salute and with a, "Right, sir!" hopped back into the trench and ran off to retrieve it.

"Happy Christmas," said the German, gripping Charlie's hand.

"Happy Christmas, sir!"

"Lieutenant Hausdiener, Karl Hausdiener."

"My name is Charlie, sir."

Now rows of British soldiers were shaking hands with Germans, and the Germans were all wishing them

a, "Happy Christmas!" or if they didn't know the English a, "*Frohe Weihnachten!*"

The foul-mouthed and foul-mooded officer they had left behind stuck his head up out of the trench and shouted,

"Toby!"

Toby spun around half-startled but quickly flashed a smile and sang out, "All the time, sir!"

The officer looked puzzled, heavy brows knitting, and said through a large, respectable, and twitching mustache, "... 'all the time'?"

"Toby, sir!" and away he skipped with a laugh. He bounded over to a young German, and clasping his hand wished him a, "Happy Christmas!" A few stutters and words Toby couldn't understand informed Toby that his new-found friend didn't speak a lick of English — not that Toby minded. The German pointed at Toby, then tugged at the ornate button on the breast pocket of his own jacket and switched his hands back and forth, lifting his eyebrow quizzically.

"Toby, sir!"

Toby understood and smiled broadly while nodding and saying, "Yes, yes, do let's!" He whipped out his bayonet without a thought and sliced off the button of his left pocket and extended it towards the German. The German eyed the large, sharply shining bayonet with an expression half entertained and half scandalized and pulling a pen knife out of one pocket snipped off his corresponding button and handed it to Toby.

"I'm Toby. Toby."

"Siegfried."

"*Fussball*!" somebody shouted, and up out of the German trenches emerged a muscular young man with a football in his hands.

"Jolly-good!" exclaimed Toby, and slapping Siegfried on the shoulder and indicating with a nod, he ran over to the group gathering.

"Brits versus Germans, Brits versus Germans," someone or other was calling, "All in good fun, lads, all in good fun!" An appropriately large space of ground was found, goals established, and soon a spirited game of football commenced. The first match was Brits versus Germans, but after that captains chose teams and it was a rollicking good way to learn a little bit of another language.

Vibert played a match or two, traded jack-knives with a German, was allowed to take a look into the German trenches (but respectfully kept it short), and then after declining several cigarettes and a cigar (Polly, as her sister Daisy, had an aversion to smoking, and so neither Vibert nor Jack smoked) joined an impromptu choir gathered beside one of the *tannenbaum* and sang,

Oh, holy night, the stars are brightly shining;
It is the night of the dear Savior's birth!
Long lay the world in sin and error pining,
Till He appeared and the soul felt its worth.
A thrill of hope, the weary soul rejoices,
For yonder breaks a new and glorious morn.

Fall on your knees, oh, hear the angel voices!
Oh, night divine, oh, night when Christ was born!
Oh, night, O holy night, oh, night divine!

So led by light of a star sweetly gleaming,
Here came the wise men from Orient land.
The King of kings lay thus in lowly manger,
In all our trials born to be our friend!

Fall on your knees, oh, hear the angel voices!
Oh, night divine, oh, night when Christ was born!
Oh, night, oh, holy night, oh, night divine!

Reaching the end, and all laughing over the Germans' struggle to sing along in English and bowing and smiling to the cheers and applause, someone suggested, "Let's go again in German!" and so they all started again,

Oh, heilige Nacht, die Sterne funkeln hell,
Es ist die Nacht in der der Retter geboren wurde!
Lange suhlte sich die Welt in Sünde und Irrtum,
Bis Er erschien und seine Seele ihren Wert erkannte.
Ein Gefühl der Hoffnung und die erschöpften Seelen
frohlocken,
Denn in der Ferne bricht ein neuer Morgen an.

Fallet auf eure Knie, oh, höret der Engel Stimmen!
Oh, göttliche Nacht, oh Nacht,
in der Christus geboren wurde!
Oh, Nacht, oh heilige Nacht, oh, göttliche Nacht!

Geführt vom Licht eines lieblich funkelnden Sterns
Kamen drei Weise aus dem Morgenland.
Da lag der König der Könige in niederer Krippe,
Geboren, um uns in allen Prüfungen Freund zu sein!

Fallet auf eure Knie, oh, höret der Engel Stimmen!
Oh, göttliche Nacht, oh Nacht,
in der Christus geboren wurde!
Oh, Nacht, oh heilige Nacht, oh, göttliche Nacht!

This time the Brits were left either stuttering along or (and this was most of them) standing there rather awkwardly and totally lost. It really threatened to kill the mood, the language barrier, but before the choir could break apart a short, middle-aged, somewhat portly, and squeeky-voiced British soldier said, "How's about *Audeste Fideles?*" And just like that Brits and Germans alike broke into clear, confident song:

Adeste fideles læti triumphantes,
Venite, venite in Bethlehem.
Natum videte
Regem angelorum:
Venite adoremus
Venite adoremus
Venite adoremus
Dominum.

They sang a few more carols, and then someone had the idea to sing back and forth, the Brits for the Germans and the Germans for the Brits. A bit of a more inviting arrangement, men felt comfortable coming and going, especially Doug, one of the men in Vibert's troop who had been a prison guard before the war. Oh, Doug was very comfortable. Eventually Vibert wandered away from the group, and found a young German officer with a kettle of something steaming.

Without a word he poured a tin cup of it and handed it to Vibert. Brown and murky, Vibert hated coffee but he couldn't be rude and a warm drink was a warm drink. He took a sip, nearly sputtered, and then broke into a wide grin.

"Chocolatte!"

The German laughed. "We had little milk, good German cow's milk." His accent made "little" sound like "leetle" and "cow's" sound like "couce" but Vibert understood him alright. "And you had schokolade. Happy Christmas!"

"*Frohe Weihnachten*!" Vibert said, imitating the phrase he had heard to his new German friend's delight. He stuck his hand out. "Vibert Trevor."

The German let out a happy exclamation, grasped Vibert's hand heartily, and nearly dropped the hot chocolatte. "Vibert too! Vibert Grossdorf!"

"Well, how about that! Where are you from, Vibert?"

"Stettin."

"Where is that?"

"Pomerania, near the sea …"

"Do you have siblings?"

"Siblings?"

"Brothers and sisters?"

"Ah. Three brothers, two sisters. Older. One sister the same as me, me …"

"Your twin?"

"Ja, ja!"

"So you're the youngest?"

"*She* is the youngest."

They both laughed.

"How old are you?"

"Nineteen," Vibert Grossdorf struggled out.

"Nineteen as well."

"You have girlfriend?"

"No," said Vibert, and the other Vibert cocked a brow. "I have a wife."

The German Vibert looked slightly deflated. "A wife?"

"We married right before I left for — here! There wasn't any time to waste and it didn't seem to make sense to wait."

"Ve had to vait," Vibert's "w"s sounded like "v"s, "but ve'll marry soon, soon as var is over."

"Grand!" Vibert said, "what's her name?"

"Maria."

"Lovely name."

"Picture!" Vibert raised a finger, "I have picture!" He handed Vibert the kettle, removed a glove, and snaked his hand into his bosom. It emerged with a leather pocketbook, from which he removed a few papers, shuffled through them, and then with a smile held one out. "Ah, Maria." Vibert sidelled up next to him and looked at the photograph with him.

"Very pretty girl."

"Ja. And you?"

"My wife's name is Polly. I think I've got a picture too," Vibert handed the kettle back and began to search his own pockets, "unless I left it in the dugout." He found it, however, and they repeated their steps.

"Very pretty," said Vibert.

"This is her in her wedding dress. They wanted to take the picture before the ceremony, but she refused, said she wanted me to carry a picture of my wife with me." They both laughed.

"No one but the wife!"

"No one but the wife!"

"You need make it home," said the German suddenly. "I do too — I vant to." He hung his head it seemed, or perhaps only looked down. "Truce, between you and me. I see you, I no shoot. You see me, you no shoot."

"It's a deal," said Vibert, and they shook on it. "Keep your head down, and we'll make it home safe."

They both looked down, feeling somewhat sheepish or awkward, and saw there lying in the snowflakes a German *Gewehr* and a British Lee-Enfield, coated in a thin dust of white. They both looked up and smiled at each other.

"My first Christmas away from home," commented Vibert, thinking of his family, father, sister, brother, wife, and all gathered at Myst Hall.

"Far from home," agreed Vibert, missing ice-skating, mother, twin sister, and his dog back in Stettin.

"But a good one."

"Happy Christmas, Vibert Trevor."

"*Frohe Weihnachten*, Vibert Grossdorf."

The German smiled and toasting the kettle went to share the rest of the *schokolade* with whomever. Vibert watched him go. "The war won't last forever," he promised softly, "the madness will end." He remembered the words of Lord Byron he had quoted earlier, and smiled up at Heaven, thanking God for hope.

Christmas '14 – our Christmas far from home. Happy Christmas – C.B.

Jack mingled a contented sigh with a puff of cigar smoke. He looked down at the *zigarre* and chuckled. He looked up at his generous and persuasive friend as he took another pull. The German laughed.

"Iz a good zigarre, no?"

"Very good. I haven't smoked in years. I used to smoke cigarettes — never had a cigar before."

"Ja? Vat made you stop?"

"My wife. Or, well, when Daisy and I were sweethearts, she told me — well, that I had better leave off smoking permanently or I would have neither sweetheart nor wife."

The German laughed. "Ze only sins in var are cowardice and cruelty," he said, toasting his own cigar to Jack, "never our comforts." He breathed out a wreath of smoke. "Few as zey are.

"Yez, my wife vill not let me smoke in ze house. So, I smoke in ze garden, or in ze club, or in ze trenches. Ha-ha! How long married?"

"Seven months."

"Ah, young pup! So no children? But young love iz a happy time. Or should be."

"My wife is expecting, actually."

"Ja! Happy day!" The German grabbed him by the shoulders and kissed both of his cheeks.

"Thank you!" Jack laughed, too in the spirit to be flustered. "Do you have children, sir?"

"No 'sir,' please, no 'sir.' Today, we are all brothers; tonight, ve are all friends. I have one daughter. Her name is Sophie. My very heart. She sent me these zigarres."

Jack laughed. "What a beautiful daughter!"

"I sent her some of our art," the German chuckled, "ve share the little zings ve know vill matter."

Jack looked at his friend, a sad smile pulling at the corner of his mouth. He looked down, looked up. Snowflakes were on the ground and in the air. The ugliness of the horrors of war were covered over in pure white, and the sadness was hidden too.

"Is it hard?"

"Hard?"

"Being away from your wife and from Sophie for so long, with the mail not even coming every week."

The German sighed.

"Sorry."

"Oh, I do not mind. You know it is difficult. But all I have to do is zink of being with zem, and ze hours just … fly by." He puffed his cigar. "As do the shells."

Jack laughed heartily. At first.

"Don't hide your tears. Ve are both far from home, in a foreign land. Surrounded by madness. It's soldiers, you and me and all of our friends, ve carry the whole var on our shoulders for the sake of our countries. Is that vy ve bury our friends?" He shook away his ash with a snap that looked like he had cast his cigar to the ground in disgust.

"We are all friends," said Jack, and the German's shoulders relaxed. "Tonight," he gestured to the whole of no-man's-land and the swaths of men conversing there, "we all walk among friends. Don't think about tomorrow. We'll all start shooting again. A few years from now, when we look back on today, we won't remember the battle, just our friends."

The German grunted in agreement and blew a smoke ring towards the sky.

"Fudge, sir!" said a bright voice, and Jack and the German blinked to find Tommy standing in front of them with a happily painted tin and an even happier grin on his face.

"Well done, cousin. Fudge, my friend? It's stale, but …"

"But Daisy makes the best stale fudge I ever tasted!"

The German raised a quizzical brow and gingerly lifted a piece from the tin, then to his eye, and then to his mouth. He smiled and toasted his cigar once again. Jack and Tommy smiled back.

"Happy Christmas!"

They wandered off into no-man's-land to share more of the tin.

"Who was your friend, Jack?"

"You know, Tommy, I didn't catch his name."

Tommy shrugged. "Fudge?"

"Spread it around."

So off went Tommy offering fudge and giving out "Happy Christmas"'s liberally. He was sixteen years old, and this was perhaps the best day of his life. He had had pleasant days, and he had had exciting days, but to be wandering in a field where even just hours before only the dead tarried for more than a few brief minutes, in a dawn illuminated by candles and lanterns, walking and talking among compatriot and foe alike freely was something entirely beyond anything he had ever experienced.

He had not yet grown up too fast - he had not yet been exposed to the full horrors of war, cooly and mercilessly subjected to its terrors by the reaper whose name is death. There were sounds that would haunt his mind in later years that he had not yet heard, scenes that would play out in waking and sleeping memory he had not yet seen. For one last day he would enjoy his youth and the illusion of the romance of war. One last day before men who laid

the rifle down willingly were ordered to take it up again. One last day where the simple soldiers could simply be brothers and friends.

Charlie was grinning, peering over the edge of a pad and putting the finishing touches on a sketch of the scene in front of him. Men drinking and smoking and singing around a little Christmas tree, two fellows, one British, one German, sharing a newspaper, a cluster of officers lighting each other's cigars, a couple of privates exchanging belt-buckles.

A German came and looked over his shoulder. Charlie turned to say hello. The other smiled back warmly, but unable to speak English could only admire Charlie's sketch. Someone had brought forth a violin and was walking through the crowd, playing an old familiar carol. Men danced and sang along.

"Do you draw?" asked Charlie, making signs with his hand. The German seemed to understand, because he pulled out a pad of his own and showed a few sketches to Charlie.

"Oh, these are lovely, sir!" said Charlie as the German showed him birds, a dog next to regimental colors (the same dog was wandering about the men, sniffing at legs and getting pats on the head), a maternal figure and the portrait of what might have been a sister or a sweetheart, and then one of a British soldier who —

"Why that's me!" exclaimed Charlie.

The German laughed mirthfully at Charlie's discovery. He tore the page out and handed it to Charlie.

"For me?"

The German only smiled.

"Wait a moment," Charlie scribbled a note on the bottom of his sketch and tore it out as well, handing it to the German. The German looked shocked, mouth gaping, staring down at the picture, up at Charlie, and back at the sketch again like it was some treasure. Charlie was happier to give it.

"Paul!" someone called, and the German's friends were waving him over to a football match. The German gave Charlie one last smile, waved goodbye with the paper, and ran off to join the game. Charlie looked after him, thanking God for this day as British and German brass joined together in playing *Let there be Peace on Earth* somewhere down the line.

Snow crunched beside Charlie, and still smiling he turned to see who it was. He was startled to see it was the officer from the trench, the one who had vowed to court martial each and every one of the cousins. Then he was surprised to see on the officer's face not a scowl, but the glistening of teary eyes. It was unexpected but rather gratifying to be suddenly embraced by the big, burly commander, and Charlie hugged him back with all the maternal instinct a brother can muster.

The officer clasped him on the shoulders and held him at arm's length. "Thank you, son."

"You're welcome, sir! ... May I ask what for?"

The officer released him and pulled something from his breast. "I have here orders," he unfolded a rather stiff piece of paper with some very official looking markings on it, "orders I was eager to follow, to the effect that if anyone, German, Brit, or Frenchie - even a Belgian - should attempt anything felicitous, or worse, *peaceful*, because it was Christmas, they were to be immediately shot, and I was to use the opportunity to kill as many Huns as possible. All by the book ..." The officer looked down at the communique, as if rereading it. "But you, my boy, you ... saved Christmas — saved me!" He looked around at the football game, the carollers, the sharers of coffee and brandy, the ones trading buttons and knives and cigarette cases, at the Christmas trees, and smiled with a sigh. "What is your name, lad?"

"Charlie, sir, Charlie Butler."

The officer smiled at him and tore the paper into pieces which he scattered in the snow. "Happy Christmas, Charlie."

"Happy Christmas, sir!"

Let there be peace on earth
And let it begin with me;
Let there be peace on earth,
The peace that was meant to be.

With God as our Father
Brothers all are we,
Let me walk with my brother
In perfect harmony.

Let peace begin with me,
Let this be the moment now;
With every step I take,
Let this be my solemn vow:

To take each moment and live each moment
In peace eternally.
Let there be peace on earth
And let it begin with me.

Lass es Frieden auf Erden geben
Und lass es mit mir beginnen;
Lass es Frieden auf Erden geben,
Der Frieden, der sein sollte.

Mit Gott als unser Vater
Brüder, alle sind wir,
Lass mich mit meinem Bruder gehen
In perfekter Harmonie.

Lass den Frieden mit mir beginnen,
Lass das jetzt der Moment sein;
Mit jedem Schritt, den ich mache,
Lass dies mein feierliches Gelübde sein:

Jeden Moment zu nehmen und zu leben
In ewigem Frieden.
Lass es Frieden auf Erden geben
Und lass es mit mir beginnen.

<u>Look out for these Releases
From the
"Christmas in the Fandom"
Series!!!</u>

Christmas at Myst Hall (1913)
Publication Date TBD

A Christmas Far From Home (1914)
Released May of 2024!

A Christmas Dark and Cold (1915)
Publication Date TBD

Christmas for Willy Redfern (1916)
Coming Christmas of 2024!

Keep the Home Fires Burning (1917)
Publication Date TBD

A Christmas When the Bells Rang (1918)
Coming Christmas of 2024!

Spotify Playlist for "A Christmas Far From Home": Christmas Truce 1914